The Baby Pony

Do you love ponies? Be a Pony Pal!

Look for these Pony Pal books:

PONY PALS

The Baby Pony

Jeanne Betancourt

illustrated by Paul Bachem

A
LITTLE APPLE
PAPERBACK

SCHOLASTIC INC.
New York Toronto London Auckland Sydney

ISBN 0-590-69776-5

Text copyright © 1996 by Jeanne Betancourt.
Illustrations copyright © 1996 by Scholastic Inc.
All rights reserved. Published by Scholastic Inc.
APPLE PAPERBACKS® and the APPLE PAPERBACKS® logo are registered trademarks of Scholastic Inc.

22 21 20 19 18 17 16   2/0

Printed in the U.S.A.   40

First Scholastic printing, May 1996

For Emily Maverick Shankman

With thanks to Robert Commerford and Maria Genovesi for sharing their knowledge of horses with me.

Contents

The Baby Pony

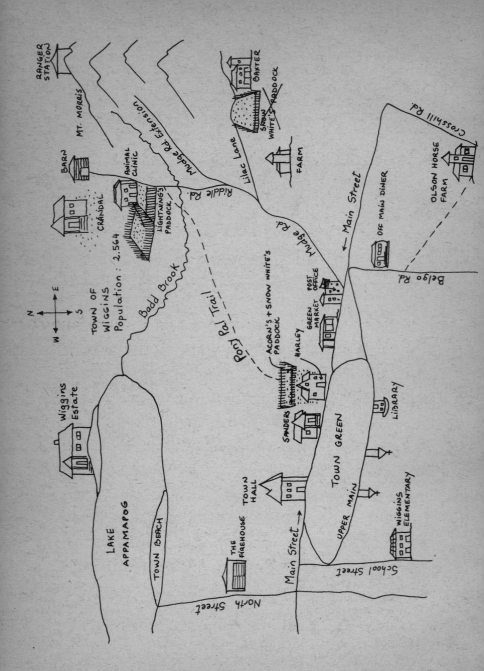

The Orphan

Lulu Sanders rode her pony, Snow White, through the paddock gate and onto Pony Pal Trail. Anna Harley followed on her little Shetland pony, Acorn. Lulu took a deep breath of the morning summer air. It was a clear and breezy day — perfect weather for a long trail ride.

Anna was excited, too. Pony Pal Trail was her favorite place in the whole world. "If we canter," she said, "I bet we'll beat Pam to the three birch trees."

"Let's go!" shouted Lulu.

As Anna rode, she thought about how wonderful it was to be a Pony Pal. Pam Crandal and Lulu Sanders were her best friends. She had known Pam since kindergarten. And even though Lulu was a new friend, Anna felt like they'd been friends for just as long. Anna was glad that Lulu lived next door and that their ponies shared the paddock behind her house.

Lulu was thinking about the Pony Pals, too. She was thinking about how great it was that they all loved being outside and learning about nature. Lulu thought that they were pretty good detectives, too. And the three girls loved adventure. But most of all the Pony Pals loved ponies.

Anna slowed Acorn to a walk. "Time to cool down," she told her pony. "I don't want you to get too sweaty. We're going to do a lot of riding today."

Anna and Lulu halted their ponies at the three birches. "We beat Pam and Lightning," Anna said.

"They'll be here in a few minutes," said Lulu.

A few minutes passed. And then ten minutes passed. But Pam Crandal and her pony, Lightning, still weren't there.

Anna was worried. Pam was never late. "Let's ride toward her place," she said.

"I bet we'll meet them on the trail," said Lulu.

But Pam Crandal wasn't riding to meet her friends on Pony Pal Trail. She was still in her family's barn. Pam knew that Anna and Lulu would be worried about her. And she knew that sooner or later they would come looking for her. She hoped it would be soon, because she needed their help.

Finally, Pam heard Lulu and Anna calling, "Pam, where are you?"

"I'm in here," answered Pam. "In the third stall."

Anna and Lulu ran down the barn aisle. "I hope she's not hurt," Lulu whispered to Anna.

Anna and Lulu found Pam sitting on a bed of straw in the stall. A bay-colored foal lay beside her.

"Oh, look," said Anna. "A foal. It's so cute."

"It's only three days old," said Pam.

The foal made a little nickering sound. Pam leaned over and rubbed its neck. "It's okay," she whispered to the pony. "I'm right here."

Lulu noticed the worried look on Pam's face. "Where's the foal's mother?" she asked.

"The mother died last night," Pam answered.

"Oh, poor baby pony," said Anna. She sat next to Pam and put her hand on the foal's side. She could feel his heartbeat against the palm of her hand.

Lulu rubbed the foal's silky brown coat.

It was the softest thing she'd ever touched. "Was his mother a patient in your father's veterinary clinic?" she asked Pam.

"No," Pam answered.

"Then how did the foal get here?" said Anna.

"A farmer brought him when I was getting ready to go meet you on the trail," said Pam. "He said that if we could keep this foal alive, we could have it for our trouble."

"Why can't he take care of it himself?" asked Lulu.

"He said he doesn't have time to hand rear a foal," answered Pam. The foal nickered weakly again.

"You poor little thing," said Lulu.

"Where's your dad?" Anna asked Pam.

"My parents are hiking with the twins today," Pam said. "I phoned my dad's beeper, but I don't know when he'll be able to call me back. They're probably on a trail by now."

"That means we have to take care of the

6

baby pony," said Anna. "How do we do that?"

"We've got to get him to drink something," said Pam. "Foals drink from their mothers all the time. This foal has to start drinking soon — " Pam finished the sentence in a whisper — "or he'll die."

Pebbles

Lulu looked at the hungry, sad foal. They *had* to find a way to feed him.

Lulu's father traveled all over the world studying wild animals and sometimes he took Lulu with him. Lulu remembered the time she and her father were in Africa together. During that trip they visited a home for baby animals that didn't have mothers. Many of those orphaned animals still needed their mother's milk. So the workers at the orphanage fed them with big baby bottles. They let Lulu hold a bottle for a baby zebra. Lulu helped feed the baby zebra at that animal orphanage. "Maybe we can get the foal to drink milk from a bottle with a nipple," she said.

"Good idea," said Pam.

"Do we give him plain old milk?" asked Anna.

"It'd be better to give him mare's milk," said Pam. "My dad sometimes has powdered mare's milk in the office. You stay with the foal and I'll go look."

"We'll need a bottle with a nipple, too," Anna called after her.

Lulu and Anna sat next to the baby pony. Lulu remembered seeing frisky foals running beside their mothers in open fields. But this foal lay alone in the straw, breathing slowly, and looking sick. Lulu felt sad for the baby pony. Lulu's mother died when Lulu was little, too. She knew what it was like to grow up without a mother. She rubbed her hand along the pony's smooth neck. "It's all right, baby," she said, "We'll take care of you. You'll have your bottle in a minute."

But when Pam came back she was holding an empty nursing bottle. "I found a bottle with a nipple," she said. "But my dad's out of mare's milk."

"Can we give him regular milk?" asked Anna.

"We could try it if we had any," said Pam. "But I finished up our milk in my cereal this morning."

Pam knelt beside the pony. She could see that in the few minutes she'd been gone, the foal had become sicker. Pam knew that if they didn't get liquids into him soon, he could die. The baby pony sighed and closed his eyes. The Pony Pals had to find him some milk.

"I'll ride to town and buy milk," said Lulu.

"That'll take too long," said Pam. "We've got to do something *now*."

"What about the twins' goat, Pebbles?"

asked Anna. "Could we get some milk from her?"

"That would be a fast way to get milk," said Lulu. "And you know how to milk her, Pam."

Pam was already on her way out of the stall. "I'll be right back," she said.

Pam rushed across the paddock toward the goat's shed. Pebbles was munching on hay. Pam liked the small goat with her floppy ears. Pam's six-year-old sister and brother fed Pebbles and cleaned the pen, but Pam and Mrs. Crandal milked her. Pam saw that there was plenty of milk in Pebbles' udder.

The goat bleated a greeting to Pam and went back to eating her hay. Pam washed her hands with soap and water at the outdoor faucet. When Pebbles saw Pam pick up the milk pail, she climbed on her milking stand.

Pam sat down at the edge of the stand. "We need your help, Pebbles," she said.

Pam washed off the goat's teats with a

soft rag. Then she took a teat in each hand and pulled down. After the first spurts of milk came out, Pam directed the warm milk into the pail. As she milked Pebbles, Pam told the goat how the milk could save a foal's life.

Back in the barn the phone rang. Lulu answered. It was Dr. Crandal. "I got a beeper call from home," he said. "What's happened? Is Pam all right?"

Lulu told Dr. Crandal all about the three-day-old foal.

"Try to get some milk into him," he told Lulu. "That's the best thing you can do for him right now."

Lulu was hanging up the phone when Pam came back into the barn with a bottle of goat's milk. Lulu followed her into the stall where Anna sat with the sick foal's head on her lap. Pam handed the bottle to Anna.

"Okay, baby," Anna told the foal. "Drink this."

Anna rubbed the nipple against the foal's

lips. But the pony refused to open his mouth. "It's good for you," said Anna. "You'll like it. I promise." Anna put the nipple to his lips again. The foal shook his head from side to side and stood up to get away from the bottle. He was tottering on his long, wobbly legs.

"I have an idea," said Lulu. "Hold the bottle so he reaches up for it. That's the way he would drink from his mother."

Anna held the bottle above the foal's head. "Here, baby," she said. "Drink some delicious milk."

The foal backed away from the bottle.

"Put a few drops on your finger," said Pam, "so he can taste it."

"You do it," said Anna. She handed the bottle to Pam. "You're the one he knows best."

Pam put a few drops of milk on her fingers and held them out to the foal. He sniffed at the fingers and licked off the drops. Pam pressed the nipple so more milk would ooze out. The foal raised his head and licked it. Pam rubbed the sides of his jaw. "Come on, little pony," she said. Finally, the foal opened his mouth and put his lips around the nipple.

The Pony Pals heard the *slurp slurp* of the foal's sucking. They smiled at one another. The foal drained the bottle. Then he nuzzled his head against Pam's side as if to say, "Thank you." Pam stroked his head. "Good foal," she said. "You drank the whole thing."

"He likes goat's milk," said Lulu.

"But he'll need more milk than we can get from Pebbles," Pam said. "It would be better for him to have mare's milk, anyway."

"Your parents are on their way home," said Lulu. "Your dad called."

"He'll know where to get mare's milk," said Pam.

The girls heard a loud neighing from outside the barn. "Snow White!" exclaimed Lulu.

"And Acorn," said Anna. "They're still saddled and tied to the fence post."

"Put them in the paddock with Lightning," said Pam. She looked down at the foal nuzzling her side. "I don't think we're going to be trail riding today."

A Big Job

Anna and Lulu went outside to take care of Snow White and Acorn. Lulu unbuckled the girth and lifted the saddle off Snow White's back. "Sorry you had to wait," she told her pony. "But there was an emergency in the barn. We had to take care of a foal whose mother died."

Anna hugged Acorn. "Oh, Acorn," she said. "I hope we can save the little foal."

"Here come the Crandals," Lulu said. Lulu looked up. The Crandal station wagon was pulling up to the front of the barn. Dr.

Crandal, Mrs. Crandal, and their twins, Jack and Jill, stepped out of the car.

By the time Lulu and Anna went back to the foal's stall, Dr. Crandal was examining him. Jill ran up to Lulu and tugged on her hand. "My goat gave milk for the baby pony," she said.

"Pebbles is my goat, too," said Jack. "And she's a hero."

Pam watched closely as her father examined the pony. He ran his experienced hand over the foal's body. Next he listened to his heart and lungs.

"What do you think, Dad?" Pam asked.

"I think we have our hands full," he said. "We have a frisky colt without a mother to nurse him."

"Can we save him?" Lulu asked.

"He's healthy enough to make it," Dr. Crandal answered. "But someone has to hand rear him. Your mother and I don't have time to do it."

"We'll take care of him, Dr. Crandal,"

said Anna. "We already gave him a bottle of milk."

"This colt will have to be fed every few hours for the next three months," said Dr. Crandal.

"We'll do it," said Lulu. "We can take turns."

"That's every few hours day *and night*, girls," said Mrs. Crandal.

"It's summer vacation," said Pam. "We can do it."

"I don't think you girls know what you're getting yourselves into here," said Mrs. Crandal. "Hand rearing a foal is very hard work. If you make a commitment to this animal, you'll have to stick to it."

The Pony Pals looked at one another and nodded.

"We promise," said Pam.

"He's adorable," said Anna. "It'll be fun."

"He's our responsibility," said Lulu.

"All right. You can take care of him for now," said Dr. Crandal.

"But, girls, we'll have to find a home for him as soon as he's weaned from milk," said Mrs. Crandal. "We're not keeping him forever."

"I know, Mom," said Pam. Lulu and Anna said they understood, too.

"I'll drive over to Farmington and pick up some powdered mare's milk," said Dr. Crandal. After he left, the twins ran off to make a hero's medal for Pebbles. And Mrs. Crandal went out to unpack the picnic lunch she'd made for the hike.

The Pony Pals stood around the foal. He was laying on the straw.

"Taking care of him is going to be a big job," said Pam.

"We'll have to make a schedule for feeding him," said Lulu.

"And take notes on how he's doing," said Pam.

"We should put all our notes together in a journal," said Lulu. "That way whoever ends up with the foal will know what he was like when he was little."

"I make lots of spelling mistakes when I write," said Anna. "I don't want to write something that we're going to show to a stranger."

Pam and Lulu knew that it was extra hard for Anna to learn spelling and reading because she was dyslexic.

"I'll help you with your spelling, Anna," said Lulu.

"I have an idea," said Pam. "We can make the foal's journal on my mother's computer. She lets us use it and it's right here in the barn office."

"I like working on a computer," Anna said. "And I'll make a beautiful cover for the Baby Pony Book, too."

Pam and Lulu knew that if Anna made the cover, it *would* be beautiful. She was a terrific artist.

"You could draw pictures in the journal, too, Anna," said Lulu.

"And we can take a lot of pictures of him and put those in the journal, too," said Anna.

The colt looked at the girls and nickered. The Pony Pals were having fun talking about the foal's journal. Now they remembered that taking care of him was serious business. Saving this orphan foal was up to them.

BABY PONY JOURNAL

Baby is 3 days old.
Entry by Pam Crandal

An orphan foal was brought to the veterinary center today. We hand him goat's milk. Now he is drinking mare's milk from a bottle. The foal is a male, which means he's a colt. (A female foal is a filly.)

The Pony Pals are taking full responsibilty for hand rearing the orphan colt. My mother is a riding teacher. My father is a veterinarian. They are giving us good advice. Besides, Anna, Lulu, and I have ponies of our own. So we already know a lot about how to take care of ponies.

The colt is bay. He has a light brown coat with a black mane and tail. He weighs about 42 pounds and is 6 hands high (24 inches). We call him "Baby Pony" or just plain "Baby." This is where Baby is staying.

Baby Pony's stall and yard

Baby Pony and our ponies' paddocks are right next to one another. Soon they will all be friends and our ponies will be like big sisters and a big brother to Baby Pony.

Here's a list of the things we have to do every day for Baby Pony.

To Take Care of Baby Pony

EVERY FEW HOURS
Feed 16 ounces milk
   (Mix 3/4 cup of mare's milk powder with 1 pint of water.)

EVERY DAY
Put clean straw in stall whenever soiled
Clean foal's bottom with baby oil
   (if necessary because of diarrhea)
Lead with a halter
Squirt iodine on umbilicus (belly button)
Brush coat with soft brush

Pony Pal Loft

The Pony Pals were busy with the little orphan colt all day long. At five o'clock, Anna had just finished feeding him. Lulu was cleaning out his soiled straw. Pam was figuring out their turns for bottle feeding the colt.

"Do you think Baby misses his mother?" Anna asked.

"He misses her a lot," said Lulu. "He will for a long time." She reached over and scratched the colt's withers. "But he's beginning to trust us."

"How's it going?" a man's voice asked. The girls looked up. Pam's father was standing at the stall gate.

"It's going great, Dr. Crandal," said Anna. She held up the empty bottle. "He's eating a lot."

"Mrs. Crandal and I will help with the feedings," said Dr. Crandal. "Put her down for midnight. And I'll take five o'clock in the morning."

"Thanks, Dad," said Pam.

"We're going to sleep in the barn," said Lulu. "If that's okay with you and Mrs. Crandal."

"That makes sense if you're taking care of this little fellow," said Dr. Crandal. "You might be sleeping in the barn office for a couple of weeks."

The Pony Pals smiled at one another. They loved barn sleepovers. It was almost as much fun as sleeping in a tent.

After Dr. Crandal left, Lulu said, "Maybe we can live in the barn for the *whole summer*."

"It will be like sleep-away camp," said Anna.

"Without counselors," added Pam.

"Too bad your mother needs her office during the day," said Lulu. "Then we could be really private."

"I've got the best idea," Pam exclaimed. "Let's move up to the hayloft. There's lots of room up there."

"And nobody else will be using it," said Anna. "It'll be just for us."

"A *Pony Pal* loft," said Lulu. "That'd be great."

Pam ran after her father to see if it was okay for the Pony Pals to take over the hayloft. She was back in a minute shouting, "He said yes!"

The Pony Pals set up the loft like an apartment. They spread out hay for mattresses and laid their sleeping bags on top of it. Then they made a table out of two bales of hay pushed together. Half bales of hay made perfect stools to go around the table.

"I'll go over to the house and ask my mother for a tablecloth," said Pam.

"See if she'll lend us an old bedspread, too," said Anna. "I have an idea for making a couch out of the rest of the hay."

While Pam was gone, Anna and Lulu tied three bales of hay together for the back of a couch. Three more bales made the seat. They used half bales for the arms.

Pam came back with a red-and-white-checked tablecloth, a flowered bedspread, and a broom.

Lulu swept the floor while Anna and Pam made an instant couch cover out of the bedspread and threw the tablecloth over their table. It was time to try out their new furniture.

Pam sat on the couch and leaned back. "This couch is *really* comfortable," she said. "And there's a great view."

Lulu sat on a hay stool and put her elbows on the table. She looked around. "This place is fabulous," she said.

Anna plopped on the couch next to Pam.

"We can put up some horse posters, too," she said.

"And your drawings, Anna," added Lulu. "You do the best drawings of horses and ponies."

"Let's bring up a big cooler with drinks and snacks," said Pam.

"It's going to be a great summer," added Lulu.

The girls heard thundering hooves. They were followed by shrieks, squeals, and loud snorts. They ran to the hayloft window and looked down at the paddock. Baby Pony was in the big paddock with their ponies. Acorn and Lightning were chasing him into a corner. The older ponies' heads were lowered. They were pawing the ground and snorting at the terrified foal.

The girls all spoke at once.

"Acorn, *stop!*" shouted Anna.

"He must have crawled under his fence," said Lulu.

"They're going to hurt him!" yelled Pam. "Hurry!"

The three girls ran to the ladder and climbed down it as fast as they could. They were all thinking the same thing — could they reach the paddock in time to save Baby Pony?

The Pony Pals ran across the paddock toward the angry ponies and the frightened colt. Pam reached them first. She grabbed Lightning's halter and pulled her away from the foal. Anna took hold of Acorn's halter. Lulu noticed that Snow White was standing a little way off. Her pony seemed interested in what was going on, but she wasn't being mean to the colt.

The colt was trembling all over. Lulu put her arms around him. "It's okay," she told him. "I'll protect you."

Don't Push!

Anna and Pam put their ponies and Snow White in the paddock on the other side of the barn. And Lulu led the foal back to his stall. Baby was safe and sucking on a bottle of milk when Pam and Anna came in.

"Is he okay?" Pam asked.

"He's had a big scare," answered Lulu. "But otherwise he's fine."

"Why were Acorn and Lightning so mean to him?" asked Anna. "I thought they'd all be friends."

"Our ponies were protecting their territory from a stranger," said Pam. "It's a normal thing for ponies to do."

"You're never supposed to put a new pony out with a group," said Lulu, "especially if it's little." Lulu understood why Acorn and Lightning had been so unfriendly to the strange pony. But she also wondered why Snow White had not been mean to him.

"I guess we're lucky Baby Pony wasn't hurt," said Anna.

While Lulu took care of the colt, Anna and Pam looked around his enclosure to see how he had escaped.

Anna squatted near the fence. "Pam, look," she said. "The ground here is all pawed up. You can see where Baby Pony crawled under the fence."

Pam knelt beside Anna. "You're right," she said. "We have to make him a better fence."

"There are a lot of coyotes around here," said Anna. "If he got out at night, he could be in big trouble."

"We can put chicken wire along the bottom of the fence," Pam said.

"That's a great idea," said Anna. "We should do it first thing tomorrow morning before we let Baby out."

The Pony Pals didn't get much sleep their first night in Pony Pal loft. First of all, they were taking turns getting up to feed the colt. Then the bats and mice kept them awake. As soon as it got dark, bats swooped above their heads and out the window. Next, the girls heard the scatching and tapping of mice running along the rafters.

"I'm not afraid," said Lulu. "But I still can't sleep."

"It takes a night or two to get used to sleeping in a new place," said Pam. "When I visited my cousin in New York City, the sound of cars and sirens kept me awake. But I got used to them."

"We should bring Fat Cat up here," said Lulu. "The mice will move out in a hurry when they see her."

"If Fat Cat was here now, she'd keep us awake chasing the mice," said Pam.

"Good point," giggled Anna.

Finally, the three girls fell asleep.

But when the sun rose, the bats swooped back into the loft. They squeaked as they found places on the rafters to hang upside down. The noise woke up the Pony Pals.

"Now the bats will sleep all day," said Lulu.

"Lucky bats," said Anna.

The tired girls dressed and went down the ladder to the first floor of the barn. It was time to take care of their own ponies. They poured oats into buckets and went out to the paddock where the ponies had spent the night. Lightning nickered at Pam as if to say, "How come you're always with that little pony instead of me?"

Pam gave her pony a hug and told her, "I miss you, too. You're still my favorite pony. And you always will be."

After the Pony Pals fed their ponies, they went to the house to have their own break-

fast. Anna made French toast. Pam and Lulu set the table and poured out juice and milk. Lulu and Pam were glad that Anna was the one cooking. Her mother owned Off-Main Diner and Anna had picked up lots of cooking tips there.

After breakfast, Pam and Lulu did the dishes while Anna rushed back to the barn for Baby Pony's next feeding.

Pam and Lulu spent the rest of the morning putting chicken wire around the bottom of Baby's fence. Anna stayed with the colt. She brushed his soft coat and sang him lullabies. When Pam and Lulu came back into the stall, they found Baby Pony and Anna sound asleep together in the straw.

Pam and Lulu sat down to rest, too. In a few minutes the colt woke up. He nudged Anna with his nose. She woke up and started to stand. But the colt tried to jump on her and Anna tipped over. "He's treating you like a pony playmate," explained Pam. Pam and Lulu couldn't help laughing. Anna laughed, too.

"Let's go have lunch," said Lulu. "We'll eat outside with our ponies. I miss Snow White."

"Good idea," said Anna. "I'm afraid Acorn will be jealous that I'm spending so much time with Baby Pony."

But when the girls started to leave the stall, Baby whinnied as if to say, "Don't leave me."

"You just ate," Anna told him.

"And you can go back in your enclosure now," said Lulu.

As the girls walked down the barn aisle, Baby continued to cry in a sad, sad voice.

"He doesn't want us to leave him," said Anna.

"Maybe we should eat in the barn where he can see us," said Lulu.

"He's getting spoiled," said Pam.

"He just wants a mother," said Lulu. "You can't blame him for that."

The girls ate their lunch in the paddock where both their ponies and the foal could

see them. In the afternoon they took ca
of Baby and spent time with their own ponies, too. Then they had a picnic supper near
the foal's enclosure.

That night the Pony Pals were so tired
they couldn't wait to go to bed. By nine
o'clock they were snug in their sleeping
bags.

"I wonder if bats and mice will keep us
awake tonight," said Lulu.

"I am so tired," said Anna, "that ele-
phants walking on the rafters couldn't keep
me awake."

Lulu and Pam didn't answer Anna. They
were already asleep.

But the Pony Pals didn't sleep for long.
They were soon awakened by the colt's
whinnies.

Lulu looked at the hands of her glow-in-
the-dark watch. "His feeding isn't for another hour," she said.

"He just wants company," said Pam.

"We can't stay with him *every minute*,"
said Anna.

"I'll go down and try to quiet him," said Lulu.

When the colt saw Lulu, he ran over and threw himself against her. Lulu toppled over. The colt lowered his head and nuzzled her. Lulu looked up into his cute face. "We have to teach you how to behave," she told him. "No one will want a feisty pony."

BABY PONY JOURNAL

Baby is 2 weeks old.
Entry by Lulu Sanders

We have been taking care of the orhpaned colt for eleven days. He is eating very well and growing strong. Dr. Crandal says he is a "fine specimen of a pony."

We have our own ponies. So when Baby doesn't need milk anymore, we are going to give him away. We will find someone who really loves ponies and knows how to take care of them. We have to find this person by the end of the summer. We won't have time to take care of a colt once school starts.

Since we are giving Baby Pony away, we decided not to name him ourselves. It will be fun for his new owner to give him a name. I hope that the person who ends up with Baby lives close by so we can visit him.

Baby is getting used to wearing a halter. And we are teaching him to walk with a lead rope. I hold the lead rope. Anna guides Baby with her arms. And Pam pushes him from behind. Baby doesn't mind. We put on his halter and lead rope three times a day.

At Two Weeks Old Baby Pony:
- nibbles at grass without eating it
- lies down a lot (Foals need lots of rest!)
- snorts when he's frightened

- paws the ground when he's angry
- flicks his tail when he's excited
- bucks when he's annoyed
- does a little jig when he doesn't get his way
- whines if we leave him alone
- pushes, jumps, and nips to get attention
- wiggles his nose when you kiss him on the cheek

Pam says we're spoiling Baby. He thinks we're his mother because we're the ones who give him milk. It's cute that Baby likes to be with us. And we all love him very much. The problem is he wants to be with at least one of his "mothers" *all the time.*

An animal raised by people can become too attached to human beings. Then it doesn't learn how to act with other animals of its breed.

Foals need to learn pony behavior from other ponies. But Baby is afraid of other ponies. And we're afraid they will hurt him. Acorn and Lightning already tried to attack Baby once.

My Pony Pals and I are thinking hard about how to solve this problem. We're going to have a meeting tomorrow to share our ideas about what to do. No one would want a spoiled pony who doesn't get along with other ponies.

Three Ideas

The next morning, while Baby took a nap, the Pony Pals went to the loft for their meeting about Baby Pony. They sat around the hay table to share their ideas.

"You go first, Pam," said Anna.

Pam unfolded a piece of paper and read out loud:

Find a nursing mare to feed Baby Pony

"What's a nursing mare?" asked Anna.

"It's a mare who makes milk because

she's had a foal of her own," said Lulu. "If we find a nursing mare, she can feed Baby."

"Doesn't the mare need to save her milk for her own baby?" asked Anna.

"If her baby dies, a mare might let another pony drink her milk," said Lulu.

"And my dad said that sometimes you can find a mare whose foal is finished nursing," said Pam. "If another foal starts nursing right away she'll keep making milk."

"It would be better for Baby Pony to have a pony or horse feeding him instead of us," said Anna. "Your idea is really good."

"Pam, wasn't your dad going to look for a nursing mare for Baby?" asked Lulu.

"He tried," answered Pam. "But he couldn't find any."

"Besides, Baby Pony is our responsibility," said Anna.

"Now we have to figure out how to find a nursing mare," said Pam.

"We can make posters," said Anna. "My idea was to make posters saying we are looking for someone to adopt Baby Pony in

September. I just did the drawing for the poster. We can put anything we want underneath."

"It could say we need a nursing mare," said Pam.

"*And* someone to adopt Baby," added Lulu.

The three girls worked together on what the poster should say. Then Pam printed it under Anna's drawing. When the poster was done, they all looked at it.

"That's perfect," said Lulu.

WANTED: NURSING MARE FOR
THREE-WEEK OLD COLT.
YOUR PLACE OR OURS.
ADOPTION POSSIBLE
CALL: 555-4362

"Let's put posters in the diner and Green Market," said Lulu. "Everyone goes to those places."

"And we'll ask Mr. Olson to put one up at his horse farm," said Pam. "Lots of people go there, too."

The three girls heard Baby Pony whinny and paw the floor of his stall.

"Uh-oh," said Lulu. "Guess who's awake?"

"He doesn't like to be alone," said Anna.

"I can't concentrate if he's unhappy," said Lulu. "Let's finish our meeting in his stall."

The Pony Pals started down the ladder.

"I wonder how long it will take to find a nursing mare?" asked Anna.

Pam jumped from the third rung of the ladder to the barn floor. "It might take a while," she said.

Lulu landed on the dirt floor beside Pam. "My idea is about what to do until we have a nursing mare," she said.

Anna jumped from the third rung, too. "What's your idea, Lulu?" she asked.

Lulu handed a piece of paper to Pam. As the three girls walked toward Baby's stall, Pam read Lulu's idea out loud.

Put Baby with Snow White. Snow White can teach him how to behave like a pony.

"But our ponies were mean to Baby," said Pam.

"Snow White wasn't," said Anna.

"I've been thinking about that," said Lulu. "I wondered why Snow White didn't chase Baby, too."

"Did you figure it out?" asked Pam.

Lulu nodded. "I remembered something that Mrs. Baxter told me when I bought Snow White."

"What?" asked Anna.

"Mrs. Baxter said Snow White had a foal before they bought her," Lulu answered. "I told Pam's mother that after breakfast this morning. She said ponies who've had foals are nicer to an orphan foal than mares who never had one."

"Lightning never had a foal," said Pam. "I guess that's why she didn't know how to act with one."

Anna opened Baby's stall door. When he saw the girls, he did a little jig of joy. They laughed at how funny and cute he looked. He ran over to them for petting.

"He's so adorable," said Anna.

Baby nipped Lulu's arm. "Ouch!" she said. "That hurts."

"Did he bite you?" asked Pam

Lulu rubbed her arm. "Just a nibble," she said. "But it pinched."

"I'm sure Snow White can teach Baby Pony some manners," said Anna. "Or no one will want to take him for their pony."

"Let's try putting him with Snow White now," said Lulu.

A few minutes later Lulu led Snow White into the paddock near Baby's enclosure. Pam and Anna were waiting for them with the frisky colt.

Pam thought Baby would be afraid of Snow White, but he wasn't. He pulled on the lead rope to get closer to the large white pony.

Snow White made a deep low whinny in Baby's direction.

"Let's try it," said Lulu. She let go of Snow White's halter. Pam and Anna let go of Baby.

Baby ran up to Snow White and stopped beside her. Snow White sniffed at the little pony.

"Look," said Anna. "Snow White likes him."

The colt lowered his head and tried to nuzzle under Snow White's belly.

"He thinks he can nurse from her," said Anna.

Suddenly, Snow White gave the little pony a push from behind. Baby slid and fell face forward on the ground. Snow White pinned back her ears and snorted.

The Baby-sitter

Baby Pony scrambled to his feet and ran over to the girls.

"Snow White doesn't like him after all," said Anna.

Baby Pony nickered to the girls as if to say, "Get me out of here!"

Lulu noticed that Snow White didn't chase the colt. She had just stood still and calmly watched him. "I don't think Snow White was trying to be mean to Baby," Lulu said.

"She was just telling him that she doesn't have milk for him," said Pam.

Anna pointed to the ground where Baby Pony fell. "There's a muddy spot here," she said. "He slipped when Snow White gave him a push to keep him from trying to nurse."

Snow White called to the colt with a low whinny. Baby Pony looked at her and then at the girls.

"It's okay," Pam told the colt. "Go play with Snow White. She's your baby-sitter for today."

The foal trotted bravely over to Snow White.

Snow White nodded her head toward the colt, turned, and galloped along the fence line. Then the little brown-and-black colt followed the white pony in a big circle around the field.

"They look so pretty together," said Anna.

After a second turn around the field,

Snow White stopped to graze. Baby Pony stopped beside her. He lowered his head to try to go under Snow White's belly again to look for milk. Snow White pinned back her ears and snorted at him. She seemed to be saying, "Don't you dare!"

The colt took a few steps away from the bigger pony and Snow White went back to eating grass. Baby tried to nurse again. And again Snow White pinned back her ears and snorted. Finally the colt gave up. He leaned over and sniffed around in the grass just like Snow White.

"Snow White's a great baby-sitter and teacher," said Anna.

"She really is," said Lulu. "I'm so proud of her."

After feeding Baby Pony and eating their own lunch, the Pony Pals put the colt back out with Snow White. It was fun to watch the young pony following Snow White around imitating whatever she did. But the Pony Pals had work to do.

Anna and Pam went back to the house

for art supplies. Then the three friends sat on their favorite rock near the paddock to make posters advertising for a nursing mare. When they finished, they watched the leggy bay colt running to catch up with Snow White.

"If someone adopts Baby Pony we might never ever see him again," said Anna sadly.

"I'll miss him," said Lulu.

"Me too," said Pam.

"Me three," added Anna.

The colt left Snow White and ran over to the paddock fence and nickered at the girls. He seemed to be saying, "Hey, I'm hungry."

Lulu looked at her watch. "Time for another feeding," she said. "It's my turn."

"Then we can all ride to town and put up posters," said Anna.

"But we can't all go," said Pam. "We can't leave Baby alone."

"I'll stay here," said Lulu. "Snow White will help me take care of Baby. And I'll groom him. He needs a good brushing after falling in the mud."

Half an hour later Pam tied the rolled-up posters to the back of her saddle, and she and Anna mounted their ponies. Anna patted Acorn's neck. "I love you, Acorn," she said. Pam and Anna smiled at one another. They were both happy for a chance to be with their own ponies.

The first poster stop was at the Green Market. They tacked a poster to the community bulletin board. Then they rode over to Lulu's grandmother's house and put up a poster in her beauty parlor. Grandmother Sanders gave them some clean shirts and shorts to bring to Lulu. "All this outdoors business," she complained cheerfully. "Lucinda is just like her father."

Next, Anna and Pam took the woodland trail that started on Belgo Road and rode over to Mr. Olson's horse farm.

Mr. Olson was on his way to the barn when the girls turned up his driveway. He waved and waited for them. Mr. Olson was always happy to see the Pony Pals. "What's up, girls?" he asked.

Pam explained that they were hand rearing a colt. "But we think it would be better for him to be fed by a nursing mare," she said.

"Your dad asked me about a nursing mare a couple of weeks ago," Mr. Olson said. "But I haven't heard of any being available around Wiggins."

Anna unrolled a poster and handed it to him. "Could you put this poster up in your barn anyway?" she asked.

Mr. Olson read the poster and smiled. "If you put these up you just might find a mare. And it helps that you're willing to give the little guy away. But do you girls know that a nursing mare might not accept a foal that isn't her own?"

"I didn't think of that," said Pam.

"Me either," said Anna.

"But we have to try," added Pam.

"You're right about that," said Mr.

Olson. "Hand-reared foals almost always turn out to be spoiled ponies."

"We know what you mean," said Pam. "He's already a little spoiled."

Anna and Pam said good-bye to Mr. Olson and went back over the trail onto Belgo Road. They stopped at Off-Main Diner, tied their ponies to the hitching post, and went in. Anna's mother was working behind the counter. "Good timing, girls," she called to Anna and Pam. "I just cut up a fresh batch of brownies." She poured the girls lemonade and gave them each a brownie.

Anna and Pam had their snack and showed Mrs. Harley the poster they'd made.

"Can we put it up in your window, Mom?" Anna asked.

"Of course," Anna's mother answered.

"Then we have to go right back to Pam's," said Anna. "We left Lulu alone with the colt for a long time already."

Mrs. Harley packed a brownie and lemonade for Lulu, while Pam and Anna put up the poster. When she kissed Anna good-bye Mrs. Harley asked, "When do you think you'll start sleeping at home again?"

"Not until we find a nursing mare for Baby Pony," Anna told her mother.

"Just pretend Anna's at sleep-away camp, Mrs. Harley," Pam said.

Mrs. Harley laughed. "It sounds more like *work-away* camp."

Pam and Anna thought that Mrs. Harley was right. So far summer vacation wasn't very relaxing.

BABY PONY JOURNAL

Baby is 3 weeks old.
Entry by Anna Harley

Baby Pony is so adorable. If you are the person who has this little pony, you are very lucky. Here are some of the cute things that he does.

1. Prances when he's happy
2. Snores when he sleeps

3. Rolls in the dirt after you groom him
4. Trips over his own feet
5. Laughs when you tickle him under the neck

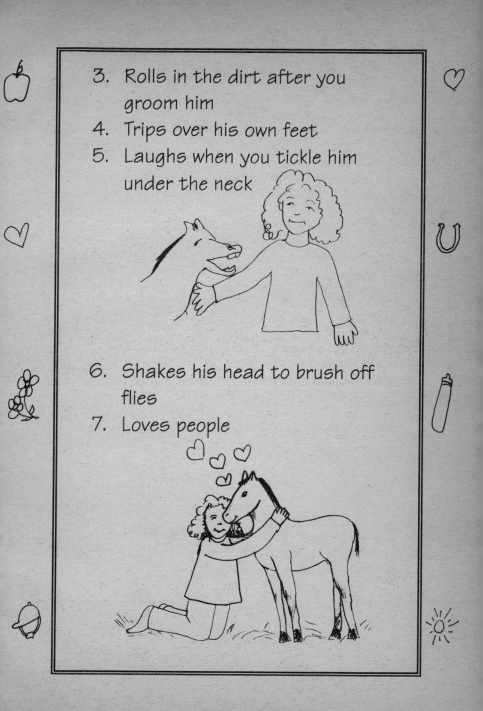

6. Shakes his head to brush off flies
7. Loves people

Lulu, Pam, and I love Baby Pony very much. We wish that we could raise him ourselves. But we all have our own ponies to take care of. We don't have time to train a foal. I hope that you will love Baby Pony as much as we do.

Here's a picture of Baby that Lulu took today.

No!

Two days had passed since the Pony Pals put up the posters advertising for a nursing mare for Baby Pony. After Baby's six o'clock feeding, Anna and Lulu played with him in the paddock while Pam mucked out his stall.

Pam had spread out a fresh bed of straw and was cleaning the water bucket when the barn phone rang. She ran to her mother's office to answer it. A few minutes later Pam came out to the paddock. The colt ran over to her and nuzzled against her side.

Pam scratched his head. "That phone call was for us," she told Pam and Anna.

"Who was it?" asked Anna.

"A woman named Victoria Winters," answered Pam. "She saw our poster in the grocery store and wants to adopt Baby. She's coming here tomorrow morning at nine o'clock. If she likes Baby she said she'd take him right away."

"How come she has a nursing mare?" asked Lulu. "Did her foal die?"

"Ms. Winters just said, 'Sand will feed him,' " answered Pam.

"*Sand*," said Anna. "What a pretty name for a horse. I bet it's a Palomino."

The Pony Pals spent the rest of the evening playing with Baby Pony. They felt sad because it might be their last day with him. That night no one complained about getting up to feed him.

The next morning the girls groomed Baby extra carefully. And Anna braided a periwinkle-blue ribbon into his mane. "For good luck," she told her friends.

At nine o'clock the girls heard a car pull up in front of the barn. They went outside. A tall, thin woman dressed in riding clothes stepped out of a yellow convertible. "It's her," whispered Anna. The Pony Pals walked over to greet her.

"I'm Victoria Winters," the woman said. "I called last night."

Pam introduced herself and shook hands with Ms. Winters. Anna and Lulu did the same.

"Now where's this foal?" Ms. Winters asked. "Do you have breeding papers on him?"

"No, we don't," said Pam.

"You can see he's a good pony just by looking at him," said Lulu.

"Baby's adorable," said Anna.

"You call him *Baby*!" said Ms. Winters. "That's no name for a horse. I hope you haven't been spoiling him."

"We're trying not to," said Lulu. "My pony, Snow White, has been teaching him pony behavior."

"Well, *my* horse, Perfection, will set him straight in the behavior department," said Ms. Winters. "He won't stand for any nonsense from a colt."

Pam wondered why Ms. Winters wasn't talking about her nursing mare, Sand.

Lulu was wondering the same thing. "What about your nursing mare?" she asked Ms. Winters. "Won't she be raising Baby?"

"I don't have a nursing mare," Ms. Winters said. "My nephew Fred Sand and I will hand rear him ourselves. *If* I think this colt is worth the trouble. Now where is he? I don't have a lot of time."

"I thought *Sand* was a horse," said Pam.

"Fred *Sand* is my nephew," said Ms. Winters. "He helps with my horses."

Anna moved in front of the barn door. She didn't like this woman. She wasn't going to let her — or her nephew — anywhere near Baby Pony.

"We aren't giving our colt away to someone who doesn't have a nursing mare," said

Pam. "Not while he's so young. It will be too hard for him to adjust."

"And we'll only give him to someone who loves horses," mumbled Anna under her breath.

"I can tell that you girls are the type who would spoil a colt," said Ms. Winters. "He will be a much better pony if I raise him. At my farm we don't spoil our animals, under any circumstances. You don't get a good price for a horse — or pony — th misbehaves."

A thought popped into Lulu's head a she blurted it out. "Do you want our colt so you can train him and then sell him for a lot of money?" she asked.

"Of course I do," answered Ms. Winters. "Why else would I go through the trouble of hand rearing him?"

"Because he's a great little pony," blurted out Anna.

"We are not giving him away to someone who doesn't want to keep him for themselves," said Lulu.

"Or to someone who doesn't have a nursing mare," added Pam.

"Oh, you silly girls," said Ms. Winters. "You're being ridiculous. A pony is just a pony! I don't understand people who are so in love with animals."

Lulu looked at Snow White grazing in the paddock. The pony sensed that Lulu was watching her. She raised her head and gave a little whinny of greeting in Lulu's direction. Lulu thought, I understand why people love animals so much.

"If this colt is really as special as you say he is, I might be willing to pay for him," Ms. Winters said. She took a few steps toward the barn door. "So let me see him."

Anna felt so angry at Ms. Winters that there were tears in her eyes. She whispered into Pam's ear. "*Don't* give her Baby."

Pam exchanged a glance with Lulu. Lulu shook her head no.

Pam remained calm and businesslike. "Ms. Winters," she said, "we are not giving — or selling — Baby to you."

Ms. Winters scowled at the girls. "Okay, okay," she said. "I see what you're doing here. If I like him, I'll give you a hundred dollars cash. On the spot."

"We don't want your money," said Lulu firmly.

Anna closed the barn door with a bang. "And we're not showing him to you," she said.

Ms. Winters glared at the Pony Pals and spoke sternly. "What a huge waste of time this has been for me," she said. She turned and got into her car without saying good-bye to the girls. The Pony Pals didn't say good-bye to her, either.

"I'd never, *ever*, let someone like that woman have Baby Pony," said Anna.

Lulu and Pam agreed.

The Pony Pals went into the barn to check on Baby. He was lying in his sunny enclosure watching a bluebird on the fence post.

"I wish we never had to give him away," said Anna.

"We may be taking care of him all summer," said Pam.

"Good!" said Lulu.

The colt saw the Pony Pals. He scrambled to his feet and ran over to them. Anna gave him a hug. "Don't worry, we won't let any mean people take you," she said.

Eve's Foal

That afternoon Mr. Olson telephoned Pam. "I just heard of a mare who might nurse your orphaned colt," he said. "I told the mare's owner about him. His name is Stan Greeley. He's on his way over to your house right now. He wants to see if his mare will accept your colt."

Pam told Mr. Olson about Ms. Winters. "Terrible woman," said Mr. Olson. "Lucky for that colt that you didn't give him to her."

"We won't give him to anyone who

doesn't really love ponies," said Pam.

"Well, good luck with the Greeleys," said Mr. Olson.

Pam thanked Mr. Olson and hung up. As Pam finished telling Anna and Lulu about the Greeleys, a pickup truck pulling a horse trailer was turning into the Crandal driveway. It pulled up to the front of the Crandal barn.

Pam saw the speckled coat of a strawberry-roan horse through the back of the trailer. Lulu noticed that a man drove the car and a young girl sat beside him. Anna thought that the girl was crying.

The man got out of the truck and walked over to the Pony Pals.

"I'm Stan Greeley," he said. "Reggie Olson told me about your colt. Our mare, Freckles, had a foal this morning. But the poor little thing was born dead. If Freckles will accept your orphaned colt, she could nurse him."

Now Anna was sure that the girl in the

pickup truck was crying. "Whose mare is it?" Anna asked.

"Freckles is my horse," said Mr. Greeley. "But the foal was for my daughter, Eve. She's in the truck. Eve is very upset that her foal died."

"I'm sorry the foal died," said Lulu.

"Me too," said Pam.

"That's so sad," said Anna.

"Maybe your mare will accept our colt," Pam said.

"You can see I brought her along with us," said Mr. Greeley. "There's no time to waste in this matter."

"I'll go get our foal," said Pam.

"I bet you've been taking very good care of that foal," Mr. Greeley said.

"We're trying," said Lulu, "but we think he's a little spoiled."

"It's hard not to spoil a foal that's being hand reared," Mr. Greeley said.

The Pony Pals smiled at one another. They already liked Mr. Greeley.

"I'll help you get your mare," Lulu told him.

Pam went into the barn. While Mr. Greeley and Lulu were opening the back of the trailer, Anna walked over to the pickup truck. She looked in through the open window. "Hi, Eve," she said. "I'm Anna. I'm sorry that your foal died."

"I loved him," said Eve. "I was going to train him and everything."

"I know," said Anna.

Pam was leading Baby Pony out of the barn.

"That's our colt," Anna told Eve. "We're going to see if Freckles will let him nurse."

When Eve saw the frisky colt, she burst into tears. "That's what my foal would have been like," she said.

"Will you help us introduce him to Freckles?" Anna asked.

"Do I have to?" asked Eve.

"It would be a big help," said Anna. "Freckles must be pretty upset that her foal died."

"Poor Freckles," said Eve. "She needs me. I have to help her." Eve was still crying, but she opened the door and climbed out of the truck.

Mr. Greeley and Lulu were backing Freckles down the ramp of the trailer. The mare was moving slowly, with her head lowered.

When Baby saw Freckles, he nickered and pulled on the lead rope.

"See, he wants to get closer to your horse," Anna told Eve.

Freckles neighed and turned back toward the trailer. She seemed to be saying, "I want to go home."

"Freckles," Eve called. Freckles looked toward Eve. The girl ran over to the horse and stroked her neck. "Oh, Freckles, I'm sad that your foal died, too," she said. "But come meet this other baby pony. It doesn't have a mother."

Mr. Greeley handed Eve a soiled rag that he was carrying. "Go rub this on the colt,"

he told her. "It has the smell of Freckles' foal."

Eve ran over to Baby Pony. The colt watched curiously as she rubbed his sides and the top of his head with the rag. He sniffed the strange smell that she was putting on him. Then he nuzzled Eve's shoulder. Anna thought she saw Eve smile.

When Eve finished putting the scent on the colt, her father led Freckles to him. Pam unhooked Baby's lead rope.

Baby trotted over to Freckles. Everyone nervously watched to see what would happen next.

Freckles lowered her head and sniffed the colt's coat.

"I hope Baby remembers how to nurse," said Pam.

"I hope I put on enough of that smelly stuff," said Eve.

"You did a great job, Eve," said Anna. "I can tell you really love ponies."

"I really do," said Eve.

Just then Freckles gave the colt a push from behind.

"Freckles," called Eve, "don't hurt him."

The Pony Pals looked at each other. What if the mare didn't accept their foal?

Lucky

Freckles gave Baby another push. Eve was about to run over to protect the foal from Freckles. But Pam put out her hand to stop her. "Wait," Pam whispered.

"I think that it's okay, Eve," said Lulu. "She's just teaching him something."

"Freckles is showing him where her milk is," said Pam.

On the third push, Baby Pony put his head under the mare's belly. Soon he was drinking milk from Freckles.

Mr. Greeley put his arm around his

daughter's shoulders. "I think we found a foal to nurse from Freckles," he said. Then Mr. Greeley looked over to the Pony Pals. "Your poster said *your place or ours*. We'd like to have the colt stay with us while he's nursing."

"Oh, yes!" cried Eve. "Please can he come with us?"

The Pony Pals smiled and nodded at one another. They didn't need to have a meeting because they were all thinking the same thing.

"Yes," said Pam. "He can go with you and Freckles."

"The poster said *Adoption Possible*," said Eve. "Daddy, can we adopt this foal? Can we?"

"Slow down, honey," Mr. Greeley said. "That depends on a few things. One being how much he costs. This might be a fancy pony."

"He's not so fancy," said Pam.

"But he's special," said Anna.

"And he's free," said Lulu. "We don't

want to make money from him. We just want him to have a good home."

"He'd have a good home with us," said Eve.

Baby Pony finished nursing but stayed close to Freckles' side. Freckles sighed happily and went back to sniffing her new colt. Baby sighed, too.

"They *really* like one another," said Anna.

"That dear little colt is *free*?!" said Mr. Greeley. "I can't argue with *that* price."

"Daddy," said Eve, "I'll take care of him just the way I would have the one who died. I will."

"I know you will," Mr. Greeley said. "And I think we should adopt him."

Eve hugged her father. "Thank you, Dad," she said. Then she turned to the Pony Pals and asked, "Can we take him home today?"

"Of course," said Pam. "They're mother and baby now."

Lulu knew she'd miss the colt. But she was happy that he had a horse for a mother instead of three girls trying to be his mother.

Anna was glad to see that Eve was smiling. Anna knew that Eve would take good care of the colt.

And Pam remembered that they had a present for Eve. "Don't go yet," she told Eve and Mr. Greeley. Pam ran into the barn. Moments later she came back out with the Baby Pony Journal. She handed the notebook to Eve.

Baby
Pony
Journal

"That's a journal we made about Baby Pony's first few weeks of life," said Anna. "So you'll know everything about him from when he was a baby."

"Thank you," said Eve. She flipped through the book. "It's beautiful."

"That's very thoughtful of you girls," said Mr. Greeley.

"Is his name 'Baby Pony'?" asked Eve. "Is that what I should call him?"

"Baby Pony is just what we called him until he got his real owner," said Pam.

"You can name him yourself," said Lulu. "He's yours now."

Eve put her arm around the colt. He looked up at her and nickered happily. "I know what I'll call him," she said. "I'll call him *Lucky*, because I'm so *lucky* to have him."

"That's a perfect name for him," said Anna.

"Perfect," echoed Pam and Lulu.

It was time for Lucky to go to his new home. He had never been in a horse trailer before. But he happily followed his new mother up the ramp and into the strange, dark space.

After Mr. Greeley closed the trailer door, he gave the Pony Pals directions to the Greeley farm. "Come visit us anytime," he said.

"Please say you'll come," Eve begged. "Lucky will want to see you. Me too."

"We'll miss Lucky. He's a very special pony," said Lulu.

"We'll visit him," promised Pam.

"We want to see you again too, Eve," said Anna.

A few minutes later the Pony Pals watched the pickup truck and horse trailer drive out of sight. "I'll always think of him as Baby Pony," said Lulu.

The Pony Pals stood silently. They were all thinking about how much they would miss the colt.

Finally Pam broke the silence. "What'll we do now?" she asked.

The question was answered by loud whinnies.

The Pony Pals turned to the paddock.

Their three ponies were standing at the paddock fence calling to them. The Pony Pals hooted and ran happily toward Snow White, Acorn, and Lightning. It was finally time for the first trail ride of their summer vacation.

Dear Pam, Anna, and Lulu,
    Thank you for giving
Lucky to me and Freckles.
Freckles loves him very much.
She's teaching Lucky to be
a good pony. Lucky doesn't
jump on people anymore.
And he's learning to eat
grass. He still rolls in
the dirt after I groom
him. But Freckles does
that, too.
    Please come see us
soon. Will you ride your
ponies here? I don't think

it is too far for you to ride them. It would be so much fun if you did. We could have a party with our ponies.

Your Friend,
Eve

P.S. Lucky still wiggles his nose when you kiss him on the cheek.

Dear Reader:

I am having a lot of fun researching and writing books about the Pony Pals. I've met many interesting kids and adults who love ponies. And I've visited some wonderful ponies at homes, farms, and riding schools.

Before writing Pony Pals I wrote fourteen novels for children and young adults. Four of these were honored by Children's Choice Awards.

I live in Sharon, Connecticut, with my husband, Lee, and our dog, Willie. Our daughter is all grown up and has her own apartment in New York City.

Besides writing novels I like to draw, paint, garden, and swim. I didn't have a pony when I was growing up, but I have always loved them and dreamt about riding. Now I take riding lessons on a horse named Saz.

I like reading and writing about ponies as much as I do riding. Which proves to me that you don't have to ride a pony to love them. And you certainly don't need a pony to be a Pony Pal.

Happy Reading,

Jeanne Betancourt

Pony Pals

Be a Pony Pal®!

❏ BBC0-590-48583-0	#1	I Want a Pony	$2.99
❏ BBC0-590-48584-9	#2	A Pony for Keeps	$2.99
❏ BBC0-590-48585-7	#3	A Pony in Trouble	$2.99
❏ BBC0-590-48586-5	#4	Give Me Back My Pony	$2.99
❏ BBC0-590-25244-5	#5	Pony to the Rescue	$2.99
❏ BBC0-590-25245-3	#6	Too Many Ponies	$2.99
❏ BBC0-590-54338-5	#7	Runaway Pony	$2.99
❏ BBC0-590-54339-3	#8	Good-bye Pony	$2.99
❏ BBC0-590-62974-3	#9	The Wild Pony	$2.99
❏ BBC0-590-62975-1	#10	Don't Hurt My Pony	$2.99
❏ BBC0-590-86597-8	#11	Circus Pony	$2.99
❏ BBC0-590-86598-6	#12	Keep Out, Pony!	$2.99
❏ BBC0-590-86600-1	#13	The Girl Who Hated Ponies	$2.99
❏ BBC0-590-86601-X	#14	Pony-Sitters	$3.50
❏ BBC0-590-86632-X	#15	The Blind Pony	$3.50
❏ BBC0-590-37459-1	#16	The Missing Pony Pal	$3.50
❏ BBC0-590-37460-5	#17	Detective Pony	$3.50
❏ BBC0-590-51295-1	#18	The Saddest Pony	$3.50
❏ BBC0-590-63397-X	#19	Moving Pony	$3.50
❏ BBC0-590-63401-1	#20	Stolen Ponies	$3.50
❏ BBC0-590-63405-4	#21	The Winning Pony	$3.50
❏ BBC0-590-74210-8		Pony Pals Super Special #1: The Baby Pony	$5.99
❏ BBC0-590-86631-1		Pony Pals Super Special #2:The Lives of our Ponies	$5.99
❏ BBC0-590-37461-3		Pony Pals Super Special #3: The Ghost Pony	$5.99

Available wherever you buy books, or use this order form.

Send orders to Scholastic Inc., P.O. Box 7500, Jefferson City, MO 65102

Please send me the books I have checked above. I am enclosing $_____ (please add $2.00 to cover shipping and handling). Send check or money order — no cash or C.O.D.s please.

Please allow four to six weeks for delivery. Offer good in the U.S.A. only. Sorry, mail orders are not available to residents of Canada. Prices subject to change. ·

Name_____ Birthdate ____/____/____

First _____ Last _____ M   D   Y

Address_____

City_____ State_____ Zip_____

Telephone (   ) _____ ❏ Boy   ❏ Girl

Where did you buy this book?   ❏ Bookstore   ❏ Book Fair   ❏ Book Club   ❏ Other   PP399